2/2014
44
3/2015

I Am King!

Written by Mary Packard   Illustrated by Leonid Gore

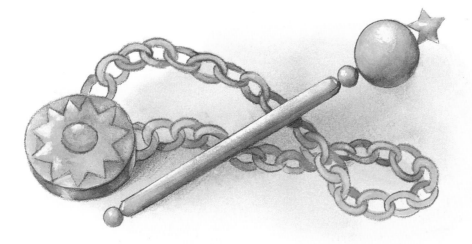

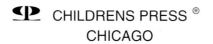 CHILDRENS PRESS ®
CHICAGO

Text © 1994 Nancy Hall, Inc. Illustrations © Leonid Gore.
All rights reserved. Published by Childrens Press ®, Inc.
Printed in the United States of America. Published simultaneously in Canada.
Developed by Nancy Hall, Inc. Designed by Antler & Baldwin Design Group.
2 3 4 5 6 7 8 9 10 04 03 02 01 00 99 98 97 96 95

Note

Once a reader can recognize and identify the 34 words used to tell this story, he or she will be able to read successfully the entire book. These 34 words are repeated throughout the story, so that young readers will be able to easily recognize the words and understand their meaning.

The 34 words used in this book are:

ahead	drum	king	see
am	everything	march	send
and	eyes	my	soldiers
army	flag	of	the
as	for	on	they
bed	hear	ring	time
come	here	run	trumpets
crown	I	say	way
do			your

Library of Congress Cataloging-in-Publication Data
Packard, Mary.
    I am king! / by Mary Packard ; illustrated by Leonid Gore.
        p.   cm. – (My first readers)
    Summary: A little boy imagines he is a king in a castle,
    commanding his army.
        ISBN 0-516-05365-5
        (1. Kings, queens, rulers, etc.–Fiction. 2. Imagination–Fiction.
        3. Stories in rhyme.) I. Gore, Leonid, ill. II. Title.
III. Series: My first reader.
PZ8.3.P125Iab 1994
(E)–dc20   94-12245
                                                                CIP
                                                                 AC

I Am King!

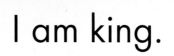

I am king.

Do as I say!

Soldiers march!

On your way!

See my crown?

See my ring?

I am king...of everything!

Hear the trumpets.

Hear the drum.

See the flag.

19

Here they come!

21

Trumpets, soldiers, flag, and drum!

Send the army on the run!

Come on, soldiers.

Eyes ahead.

Come on, king.

29

Time for bed!

About the Author

Mary Packard is the author of more than 150 books for children. Packard lives in Northport, New York, with her husband and two daughters. Besides writing, she loves music, theater, walks on the beach, animals, and, of course, children of all ages.

About the Illustrator

Leonid Gore was born in Minsk, USSR. After he graduated from the Art Institute in Minsk, he worked as an illustrator for various book, magazine, and newspaper publishers. In 1991, Gore and his wife, Nina, immigrated to the United States. He is now a permanent resident of the U.S.A., and lives in Brooklyn, New York.